MARMADUKE... AGAIN?

by BRAD ANDERSON

SCHOLASTIC INC.
New York Toronto London Auckland Sydney Tokyo

Marmaduke Again?

ISBN 0-590-09085-2

20 19 18 17 16 15 14 13   4 5 6 7 8/8

"Did I say STRIKE? How ridiculous of me! Of course I meant BALL!"

"Oh yeah? Come up here and say that!"

"Has anyone seen my toothbrush?"

"Here comes Marmaduke with another
delinquent dues payer!"

"But it's only a *slightly* cheaper brand!"

"We shouldn't have let him see that
performing bear on television."

"Marmaduke, where is Phil?"

"When I said, 'good night,' I was talking
to my wife...NOT you!"

"Each day we play a different game.
Today he has a stamp on his nose, and
insists on being mailed!"

"Keep up a steady stream of hamburgers —he's being rewarded for getting Mr. Winslow out of a traffic ticket!"

"So we're seven men short! Marmaduke
will play first, second, third, and the
whole outfield!"

"How much longer are you going to
carry on this strip-mining operation?"

"It took Marmaduke to show the Post Office how to speed up mail delivery."

"I dread this meeting. He hasn't seen me
for a week."

"Now, we're going to be gone all day.
Promise you won't cheat."

"Stop here! Marmaduke's put his
brakes on!"

"Marmaduke has a job at the movies. He cleans up all kinds of goodies on the floor."

"Dad, I think Marmaduke jumped on
your new waterbed."

"Now, don't YOU look adorable!"

"Don't get excited, Marmaduke. The sound of these pans means I'm putting them away."

"This is as good a time as any to start my
vacation!"

"Carrying the telephone book won't get
you into school."

"Where's that awful racket coming from,
Phil?"

"He's the only dog in the world that can ruin a whole room just by wagging his tail."

"We find we collect THREE times as
much as we used to!"

"Can't he just window-shop for a few minutes?"

30

"We were having a wonderful time, but
that wasn't good enough for you! You
had to stir up some excitement!"

"Oh, no!"

"I wish you two would snore in the same key!"

"I'm doing just fine, but would you
please keep my assistant out of the
kitchen!"

"I'm sorry, but I don't practice group
medicine."

"Can't you ever wade in a little at a time?"

"Don't take any with bites in them.
Those are the ones Marmaduke
sampled."

"Here comes Little Red Riding Hood
wandering through the woods and you're
the big, bad, hungry wolf! Now put some
feeling into it!"

"He's a great ball-carrier carrier."

"What do you suppose a bark like that
does to an ant's tiny eardrums?"

"He wants to make sure I get every drop
that's coming to me!"

"Our satellite in the sky has come through again! He's sighted the ice cream truck!"

"That does it! I'm turning in my badge!"

"Who put you up to this? I sent you for
my slippers!"

"Wouldn't you know he'd be the only
one with a perfect attendance record?"

"Why can't you just wag your tail the
way other dogs do?"

"Consider yourself lucky. Lots of people can't even find a doctor to treat them!"

"We don't pick up hitch-hikers and you know it!"

"You've got to stop licking dog food
commercials!"

"It's a radio. There ain't no picture."

"Now you'll see him do his famous
imitation of a lawn sprinkler."

"He just brought me my paper, pipe, and slippers...what's he done?"

"This always happens when he looks at
Billie's comic books."

"He doesn't think his dog food was
supposed to go up in price!"

"You'll just have to get another cart for
the groceries, Phil."

"I'm glad you came!"

"We appreciate your keeping him
company all day, *but*..."

"He wouldn't let us neglect him even if
we wanted to!"

"Don't say anything. Bubble gum keeps
him from barking."

"Look, you do your thing! I've had it!"

"Those aren't my slippers!"

"I can't imagine how this found its way
into the fondue pot, can you dear?"

"I don't know where he lives, but he shows up with his dish every time we have a cookout."

"Don't let Marmaduke take our candy
while we're praying."

"Don't let Marmaduke have any more snowballs! He's stockpiling them in the house!"

"I said your ear muffs are NOT in the hamper!"

"I dread it when the gum ball gets stuck."

"Cheer up. The bandages in her nurse's
kit should be used up soon."

"Mommy, is the baby's bottle warm
now?"

"I wish you'd stop giving me these
household hints!"

"Well, maybe no punishment this time,
Billy...but don't let it happen again!"

"Marmaduke got kicked out of the library for popping his bubble gum."

"The kids were practicing first aid and
we decided to let you take off the
adhesive tape!"

"Whatever you do fellas, don't mess
with this violin case. It's full of
Marmaduke's bones!"

"I'm sharing my bed with Marmaduke tonight...he gets the top berth and I get the lower!"

"What do you think this is...the
Y.M.C.A. pool?"

"Mrs. Snyder gave him some of her cookies and now he's brought me her recipe."

"He means well."

"You look guilty — even from that end!"

"Marmaduke ate the cookie before we
could tell him it was made of mud!"

"How was I to know he didn't have any money?"

"Now are you satisfied?"

"I think it's one of your relatives."

"Don't believe him, he's a
hypochondriac."

"Didn't I tell you last night there would
be no more midnight walks?"

"*NOW*, let's try that chorus again."

"It's a new version of 'fetch.' Ready?
See, now I'm mailing this stick to
Mexico!"

"I don't think we'll have to worry about
colds and sniffles this winter."

"Let me in! You didn't tell me this morning that you were changing the password."

"I'm swearing off TV until they stop
showing dog food commercials!"

"I'm hurrying as fast as I can!"

"He always does that after barking all day."

"He keeps trying to get the last bark!"